D1226284

The Wordless Weaver

Claudia Cangilla McAdam

Illustrated by
Caroline Baker Mazure

Our Sunday Visitor
Huntington, Indiana

Our Sunday Visitor Publishing Division
Our Sunday Visitor, Inc.
200 Noll Plaza
Huntington, IN 46750
www.osv.com
1-800-348-2440

ISBN: 978-1-68192-484-7 (Inventory No. T2370)
1. JUVENILE FICTION—Religious—General.
2. JUVENILE FICTION—Holidays & Celebrations —Easter & Lent.
3.RELIGION—Christianity—Catholic.

LCCN: 2020944346

Cover and interior design: Lindsey Riesen
Cover and interior art: Caroline Baker Mazure

PRINTED IN THE UNITED STATES OF AMERICA

With love for my granddaughter Elizabeth,
who brings more joy to my life than words can say.

C. C. M.

. . . . .

For Derek and Matilda, who inspire everything I do.

Caroline Baker Mazure

"My mouth is filled with your praise,
and your glory all the day."

Psalm 71:8

The young weaver Shira gripped the hands of her little brothers as the three of them squeezed through the crowd. She had to make sure they didn't get separated.

Hundreds of people lined the road winding into Jerusalem. The crowd smelled of dust and dogs, soil and sweat. They waved palm branches and blanketed the road with their cloaks.

Cymbals crashed together. The mob chanted and sang. One of Shira's brothers shouted, "Hosanna in the highest!"

The other brother added, "Blessed is he who comes in the name of the Lord!"

Shira didn't utter a word, because she had never been able to speak.

Shira spotted Yeshua riding a donkey. The Master, the Teacher, the rumored Messiah wasn't traveling on a war horse, but a humble beast of burden. And he was coming to her city for Passover!

She wanted to laugh with joy along with the crowd or join them in a hymn, but she could only smile and wave.

All the next day, as she labored at her loom, she remembered how Yeshua had looked directly at her with tenderness. The memory sent shivers down her spine.

She recalled what people said about him. He cured the sick, raised the dead. Could he heal her? If only she could have asked for her miracle.

Her fingers flew over the cloth as she worked. She wove the fine fibers into a herringbone pattern, the strands interlocking as tightly as a hug.

The mute girl was known throughout Jerusalem for her skill as a wonderful weaver. But she would gladly have traded her talent for a mouth that could shout with the loudness of a lion's roar or whisper with the softness of a morning breeze.

When her brothers recited from the Law and the Prophets, she longed to proclaim passages she had committed to memory, but her twisted tongue refused.

When her mother crooned the words of a psalm with the sweetness of a cooing dove, Shira's soul sang along in silence.

At bedtime, her father blessed each of his children. She ached to answer his prayer with an "Amen." Instead, she offered wordless worship in her heart.

Finally, Shira finished the long length of woven white cloth. It rivaled the best linen produced by the master weavers in far-off Syria.

"It will bring a good price in the market," her mother said. "We will take it there on the first day of the week."

The next morning, her mother's shrieks jolted Shira out of bed. News had come that Yeshua had been arrested and was being crucified on the hill outside the city's western wall.

Shira bolted barefoot from the house, racing along the lane and through the gate in the huge stone wall. The ragged flagstones bit at her feet, but that pain could not match the hurt in her heart.

For hours she knelt beneath the cross on the hilltop. Silent sobs shook her body. She wanted to wail or plead or pray aloud, but she could make no noise.

Yeshua's young disciple, John, slipped his arm around her shoulders to comfort her. She looked up to see agony etched in his eyes.

The sky grew black, the heavens opened, and raindrops lashed her face, mingling with the tears on her cheeks.

Yeshua was dead. The men gently lowered his body from the cross into the arms of his mother.

One older man looked at John and said, "We will lay him in my tomb, which has just been carved from rock. But where will we get a shroud to wrap him in? The Sabbath is nearly here. The shops are closed."

They needed a long length of cloth. Shira knew she could help. She touched the man's arm and then laid her hand over her heart.

"You, child? You can get the cloth for us?"

She nodded.

She raced back to her home in the city and then returned to the hillside, the newly made linen cloth clutched to her chest.

The men cut a strip of fabric from the long side of the cloth. They positioned Yeshua onto half of the linen and drew the other half up over his body. They tied the strip about his feet and wound it around and around him, knotting it at the top.

Shira watched them carry her Lord away. Her mouth opened in a soundless scream.

Sadness dulled the next day. Shira couldn't eat. She couldn't smile. She could only mourn.

On the third day, a loud pounding rattled the door. It was John.

"He is risen!" he exclaimed. He held out the shroud to her. "This was all we found in the tomb this morning." He stretched out the material. The torn-off strip of cloth was still knotted at the bottom, looped around and around the middle, and tied at the top.

Shira slapped her hand over her mouth. The cloth bore the faint image of the crucified Lord's entire body!

"You made this," John said. "Can you mend it? Sew the strip back on?"

Shira's face brightened like a sunburst. She gathered the fabric into her arms and buried her face in its folds, weeping with joy.

"May Our Lord repay you for the kindness you have shown him," John said.

He rested his hand on her head and recited the prayer her father uttered over her every night: "The Lord bless you and keep you. The Lord make his face to shine upon you and be gracious to you. The Lord lift up his countenance upon you and give you peace."

Shira sucked in a sharp breath. She tingled from the power that suddenly surged through her. Her response to John's blessing bubbled up in her chest, danced on her tongue, and then burst past her lips: "Amen!"

Background on the Shroud

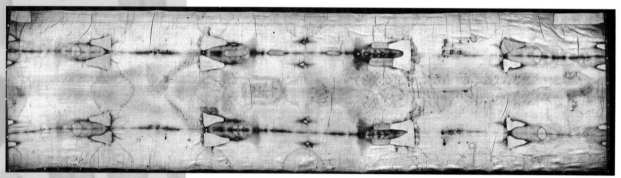

The Shroud of Turin

THE WORDLESS WEAVER is a fictional story about something that really existed: the length of cloth (called a shroud) that Jesus was wrapped in for burial.

We know that a shroud was used because Sacred Scripture tells us that, on the morning of the Resurrection, "Simon Peter and the other disciple, the one whom Jesus loved," ran to the tomb and "saw the linen cloths lying there," and when the unnamed disciple (believed to be the Beloved Disciple, John) went into the tomb, "he saw and believed" (see Jn 20:2–8).

Today, in the town of Turin in Italy, there is a very special linen cloth kept in the cathedral. It appears to be the burial shroud of a crucified man, and it measures about 14 feet long by about 3 feet wide. It shows the entire body, both front and back, and it is hundreds of years old.

The Shroud of Turin presents the image of a man who was scourged, crowned with thorns, and whose right side was pierced. Many people believe it to be the cloth in which Jesus was wrapped following his crucifixion.

Tests have been conducted on the shroud, but no one has been able to determine how this image—which appears to be similar to a photographic negative—was made on the cloth. It is not made with paint, and the image doesn't penetrate the fibers of the cloth. Rather it remains on the very top layer. If it is the burial cloth of Jesus, could the energy produced at his Resurrection have left this image?

The triangle-shaped markings on the shroud are patches that were used to repair the shroud when it was damaged in a fire in 1532.

Along the top edge of the shroud (as seen in the photo on the previous page), a seam about three to four inches wide can be seen running the entire length of the fabric. Could this strip have been torn off and used to bind the shroud around the body inside, as was the custom? If so, and if this is the burial shroud of Jesus, when he rose from the dead, there would be no need to untie the strip and unwrap the body. He would simply pass through the fabric, leaving the shroud tied with the winding strip. Is this what John saw — the undisturbed, still-bound shroud absent the body he had seen placed in the tomb — that cemented his belief in the risen Lord?

The Catholic Church has custody of the shroud but has never formally accepted or rejected it as being the burial cloth of Jesus. In 1998 Pope Saint John Paul II said of the cloth, "The shroud is an image of God's love as well as of human sin. … The imprint left by the tortured body of the Crucified One, which attests to the tremendous human capacity for causing pain and death to one's fellow man, stands as an icon of the suffering of the innocent in every age."

In 2010, Pope Benedict XVI described it as "an Icon written in blood, the blood of a man who was scourged, crowned with thorns, crucified, and whose right side was pierced."

Whether or not the Shroud of Turin is truly the burial cloth of the Lord, everyone can follow what Pope Francis has said about it: "The Man of the Shroud invites us to contemplate Jesus of Nazareth." And in so doing, each person can bring his or her own faith to the examination of this most extraordinary relic.

About the Author

Claudia Cangilla McAdam is an award-winning children's author with a master's degree in theology. She loves Sacred Scripture and has always wondered what it would be like to live at the time of Jesus. Many of her books invite children to enter into those Bible stories with her. For a free discussion and activities guide for this book, visit www.ClaudiaMcAdam.com.

About the Illustrator

Caroline Baker Mazure is a visual artist with a bachelor's degree in Studio Art from the University of Dallas and a master's degree in Print Media from Cranbrook Academy of Art. In addition to her personal art practice, she teaches K–12 art in Michigan, where she lives with her husband and daughter.